# THE DREAMER'S DREAM

## How You Buy a Small Piece of America and Profit from It

**FRANCES CASALES POTTER**

&

**FRED T. POTTER**

FRANCES CASALES POTTER

FRED T. POTTER

@2023

# Disclaimer

It is important to remember that past performance may not be indicative of future results. Several types of investments introduced to you may involve a certain degree of risk. There can be no assurances that the future performance of any specific investment, strategy, or product referred to directly or indirectly in this publication will be profitable, equal any corresponding indicated historical performance level(s), or be suitable for your portfolio. Due to several factors, including changing market conditions, the content may not be applicable to you or reflective of current opinions or positions. However, you should not assume that any discussion or information contained in this publication serves as the receipt for, or as a substitute for, personalized investment advice from Marika investments LLC" To the extent that a reader has any questions regarding the applicability of any specific issue discussed above to his/her individual situation. The reader is encouraged to consult with a professional advisor of their choice.

# Dedication

I dedicate this book to the millions of immigrants from all over the world who came to the United States with the dream of seeking opportunity and progress. Especially to the 1.5 million plus immigrants which were brought into this country by their parents at a young age, as my parents did to me, which do not know any other country as their own. To these immigrants, this country is where they were raised, received an education, and have raised families of their own. Many of these dreamers have busiensses and are productive individuals in the country.

This book is dedicated to Seyi J Ogunbamise, Wale A Ogunbamise, Marco Jose Aldrete, Nadia Amor Aldrete, and Sabrina A Rangel Aldrete, who are all my cherished grandchildren. May it serve as a heartfelt tribute to the love and memories shared, and bring inspiration and joy to each of them on their journey through life. To Marco, who has passed on, this book serves as a lasting reminder of his life and the impact he made.

# Table of Contents

Disclaimer .................................................................................... iv

Dedication ..................................................................................... v

Introduction To The Reader About This Book ........................... viii

Introducution of the Author ......................................................... ix

Chapter 1  History Repeats Itself .................................................... 1

Chapter 2  The New Entrepreneurship In Me Begins! .................... 4

Chapter 3  The Entrepreneurship Lessons Continue ....................... 7

Chapter 4  A New Chapter In My Life ......................................... 10

Chapter 5  The Cheap and Cheerful Project Continues ................ 14

Chapter 6  Scouting to Find Your Land ........................................ 17

Chapter 7  Funding and Purchasing your Future Retirement ....... 21

Chapter 8  Taking it to Completion: The Purchase ...................... 25

Chapter 9  Project begins The Vision of Success! ....................... 27

Chapter 10  Marketing Begins Sales and Cash Flow ................... 31

Chapter 11  The Documents ......................................................... 33

Chapter 12  The Sales Contract The Best Part of the Project ...... 36

Chapter 13  Tracking Your Sales And Client Payments .............. 38

Chapter 14  It All Comes Together ............................................... 40

SOME FINAL THOUGHTS ............................................................41
SUBDIVISION PLATS ..................................................................42
SUMMARYs OF INVESTMENT ANALYSIS .............................48

# Introduction To The Reader About This Book

I like to give the reader the reason for this book is to share some of my humble beginnings and some of my first experiences in coming to the United States as an immigrant and a dreamer at age 8. Also, share What it takes to reach your goals, takes challenging work, determination, and persistence to accomplish your dream without losing sight of the result.

In the book, I am giving you valuable information Step by Step on How You can buy a small piece of America and Profit from it.

By creating Owner finance subdivisions, a mailbox business, by helping people with no credit and Minimum funds to reach their dream of owning their own piece of land in America!

# Introducution of the Author

First, let me be clear. I am not a writer. I do this because this is The Great United States! The Land of opportunity for all!

I was Born on a small Mexican rancho located in the Ejido of Guerrero Coahuila, Mexico, from parents of humble beginnings, with minimal education. They were the initial dreamers who dared to venture and immigrate to the Land of Opportunity.

I remember in my early years that my parents would take me to town to visit my grandparents, riding a horse cart loaded with firewood for them to sell.

As I was talking to my ninety-four-year-old mother, she was telling me the story of how they would make the trip.

They would load their "Guallines" (wagons) with wood to sell and meet other "Guallineros" (Waggoneers) from the surrounding ranches loaded with wood, and their families would meet at three am in the morning along the roadside.

They would all line up in a caravan style, ready to ride to town. As they rode along, my mother said, "All you could hear in the dark of night was the "Balancines" or the rockers of the wagons and the trotting of the horses' hooves on the hardened ground.

The Guallineros ("rancheros") and my father would make a weekly trip to take the wood they cut during the week to sell in

Piedras Negras at an old general store called "CASA MARINES" They would sell their wood, buy their groceries for the week and of course their bottle of "MESCAL LICOR.

Once they finished their business, they would all part ways, end my parents would go to visit my grandparents. (As shown in the cover picture of wagon outside her house with Dad, Mom, and me in the back of the wagon).

The Guallineros became incredibly famous in the Coahuila area, and I am proud to say, my father, Francisco Chavez Cardenas, was one of the "GUALLINEROS from the Ejido of Guerrero

Coahuila Mexico. The Morales family's grandfather also rode the GUALLINES" One of the Morales family members composed and recorded a song, "CORRIDO LOS GUALLINEROS," to tell their story. Soon after, my parents moved from the ranch to town and started planning to immigrate to the US. Thank GOD for that, had I stayed in Mexico, I believe with my entrepreneurial spirit, I would have been selling "Chiclets under the bridge" (like are see the young children do as we cross from Mexico), trying to help their parents make a living.

I consider myself a "Dreamer" for several reasons, mainly because when I was brought from Mexico at the age of 8 years old by my parents, with the help of an uncle, Daniel Chavez Cardenas, who was already in the US. He provided the work letter required for my father at the time of immigration to allow my father to obtain a legal Visa. We all obtained our US Citizenship.

During the first six months in the US, my dad, Francisco Chavez Cardenas, and my Mother, Dolores Chavez, were invited by a relative, my mother's cousin, Mr. DeLeon, to go up north to Colorado to work in the fields with the promise of making a lot of money. However, just as it is done to many newcomers who come to the United States, the relative took most of my father's money and only gave him a small portion of what he was paid to buy the basic needs. The rancher whom they worked for noticed that my parents were extremely hard workers, so he started paying them extra on the side. With those extra funds, my parents were able to put together enough money to return to Texas; six months later, my parents had put together enough money to buy a 1938 automobile. In 1954 this was not an antique, only a basic means of transportation; that old car was all they could afford to buy to get us back to Texas.

My parents loaded their belongings, a small dog, and their little girl (me), and the Colorado adventure ended.

I am so thankful for my parents Francisco and Dolores Chavez, for bringing me to the US. They came looking for opportunities and a better future for their family.

He also taught me the same work ethic he had; he would say, "regardless of how hard the work is, do the best you can and get it done. Never Quit!"

He would also say, "Take pride in what you do. Be honest and stay focused on your short- and long-term goals; The Sky is the Limit!"

The reason I mention my parent's story is because when immigrants first come to the United States, they have stories like my parents that happened to them. Many are under the impression that immigrants come to the United States to do harm; not all immigrants are bad people; most are hard workers and productive individuals, especially working in the fields, with immense help to the farmers.

On November 6, 1986, then President Reagan signed into law Legacy amnesty for illegal immigrants. When this law was put into place, the ranchers and farmers, as well as the Dreamers seeking work, helped each other. The fields were worked, and people made a living doing jobs that most Americans and others refused to do, like picking tomatoes and potatoes and cleaning hog pens.

Immigrants are willing to work hard, long hours for small wages.

When immigrants first come to the US, they depend on their children to translate for them. I was brought to the US at the age of eight years old, and I remember I had just started going to an American school. So, with my broken English, I was the interpreter for my parents. I helped them to communicate, whether it was to apply for jobs or purchases where they needed to communicate in English what they wanted.

I have seen the same stories in my insurance business with the children of my clients; Children help their parents to translate English to Spanish just as I did to help them understand what they are buying.

After our first experience in Colorado, my father started working as a truck driver, first hauling cattle and then driving for Coca-Cola. After twenty years of working for various companies, he retired from driving trucks; soon. After, he owned and worked a Texaco gas station and a U-Haul Rental until he retired again at an older age.

THE DREAMER'S DREAM

# Chapter 1
# History Repeats Itself

I was lucky to have the good fortune of having well-educated, professional uncles, like My uncle Saul Chavez Cardenas, who was a lawyer in Mexico City, my Aunt Inez Chavez Rodriguez, and my grandparents, Daniel J Chavez, a railroad conductor and Obdulia Chavez Cardenas, a retired teacher, who taught me and corrected me so that I learned to speak and write fluent Spanish. I was told and advised that as I grew older and started seeking a career or job, it would become a tool to help me advise in any position that required me to be bi-lingual. I was told I would have better opportunities for higher salaries and advances in my career.

When we have traveled to Europe, It was amazing to see many people speaking three or four foreign Languages; restaurant servers and cab drivers where fluent in various languages and can communicate easily with traveling tourists from all over the world.

It is sad that many children and adults today do not want to speak Spanish or other native languages, fearing they will be discriminated against or embarrassed for doing so. Parents should be proud and teach them so that they can have the best of both worlds like I had the opportunity to have.

Both the American and Latino cultures are great tools and

# FRANCES CASALES POTTER

assets to have in business for a job.

I started my working career at the age of fifteen, working in a children's shop called Tots and Teens, the owner was Mrs. Beard, and as I was working for her, she taught me to do bookkeeping for the husband's car lot next door, Beard's Motors. Since this was my first job, the salary was small, but the experience and lessons learned were great. They saved money, and I learned.

After that job, I was able to help my father at his Texaco gas station with the bookkeeping.

My Sales Experience expanded into many areas; soon, I figured out sales were my strength; by being in that field, I could get paid better salaries and make decent money.

I was married at age twenty and had my first child, Mariza, at twenty-one. I continue working in sales, selling wigs door to door.

In my early twenties, I received a great offer to work for Zale's Jewelry. They had just opened a store in Eagle Pass, and they needed sales to help. I started working for a commission, and the pay was great! Especially in high-dollar jewelry sales. I worked for Zale for five years. I also worked at First National Bank in the drive-in window as a teller for a few months. While doing other jobs, I raised two daughters, Mariza Casales Aldrete and Erika Casales Ogunbamise. I worked part-time in a family-owned Antique store for 16 years, along with my 93-year-old father-in-law. My job there

# THE DREAMER'S DREAM

was sales, restoring pieces of old furniture, and delivering purchases to clients when there was no one else available to do it. While working in the antique store, in 1973, our first land development was started, and it was called Las Haciendas Subdivision.

# Chapter 2
# The New Entrepreneurship In Me Begins!

It was during these times while working in the store I started working on the development of the first Subdivision, "LAS HACIENDITAS." Among all my endeavors and jobs as we were starting the first Subdivision while getting it to take off to create another other income. I started manufacturing Bridal Accessories in a Company I named "Bridal Accessories by Fay" retail and a wholesale business in a partnership called ECO Enterprise, Esquenazi, Casales & O'Brian. We had a second-floor showroom at Dallas Market Center for seven years showing our own wedding accessories that were being manufactured in Eagle Pass, Texas. I also opened two retail stores, "Bridal Accessories by Fay," selling complete Bridal packages with accessories; those packages were being manufacture for the wholesale and retail businesses in the same building of one of the retail stores in Eagle Pass.

The second retail store was in San Antonio, selling the same Bridal packages as the one in Eagle Pass.

These businesses were started during the "OIL CRUNCH" in 1985 and the Peso devaluation in 1986. Everyone in the area that was in business along the border depended on the Mexican trade coming across the border to shop for their needs. When the monetary crisis occurred, we all looked to do business outside the area with the hope that we could make up for losses from the Mexican clientele and walking traffic across the border from Mexico.

Even though we had already started working on the first owner finance project, "LAS HACIENDITAS," in 1973, I continued doing other jobs to create some income until the land sales took off. The first project, once started and completed, did not take long for it to pay for itself, the expenses, improvements, and a salary for me.

Shortly thereafter, I only had to work on the owner-finance land development. Based on the success of that first Subdivision, Las Haciendita, we started looking for land to do the second Subdivision, called "Las Carretas, "owner finance land sales. We went ahead and followed the steps just as we did with the first owner-financed land development with Mailbox income, the same as the other subdivisions that have already proven to be a successful outcome.

We then started looking for land to develop the third project by following the same steps to develop as before in the other two subdivisions. The third development was started called "La Herradura. I will explain in more detail in later chapters the complete process and show with examples of Summaries and

Surveys to give you a better idea of our projects, the process, and the profits.

Going through the crisis of 1985-1986 of the peso devaluation and the "OIL CRUNCH" it helped us to see that this business is recession-proof. Regardless of the economy, we are serving need to these kinds of land Buyers that are in need of a home, especially in areas where there is a shortage of rentals.

These kinds of buyers need affordable monthly payments and a small down payment. Most of these clients have little or no credit. This is what makes the owner's finance business so valuable and profitable; interest is charged and added to the monthly payment; it is a WIN-WIN! For all.

# Chapter 3
# The Entrepreneurship Lessons Continue

My focus became totally on the affordable land development/ owner finance business, with the guidance, direction, and Ideas from my mentor, my 93-year-old father-in-law, Jose Casales Sr.

We started the first project, LAS HACIENDITAS Subdivision. The idea was to seek land to develop and find a property that the owner was willing to finance. An owner would also need to be willing to negotiate the terms of the owner's financing agreement and get paid monthly payments, and to be willing to release parts of the land when purchasers wanted to pay off their land early.

The first Subdivision we bought was 33 acres (half the area of The Vatican) out in the country (about half the area of a large shopping mall) in Eagle Pass. It was purchased from the children of a late Sheriff Salinas from Eagle Pass. His children had inherited the land and the oldest son, Sabino Salinas, was the executor of his father's will; he was the one we negotiated the purchase with for those acres that became our first owner financed Subdivision called "LAS HACIENDITAS." At the time, acreage could be divided into lots, and most lots were about 100 feet by 150 feet, which produced a total of 107 lots.

# FRANCES CASALES POTTER

In 1977, we started our second project using the same owner-finance concept. We named it "LAS CARRETAS," and it was also owner financed, and this acreage produced asserted sizes with a total of 97 lots.

In 1978, we bought 66 acres outside the city limits, which became the "LA HERRADURA" Subdivision; it was our third owner-financed project. By using the same concept of the earlier two owner finance and mailbox income subdivisions same as we did before, this acreage produced lots of many sizes with of a total of 311 lots. This brought our grand total of 405 lots. From 1973 through 2003, the payments continued from the clients and brought in a total income of 5 million dollars in principal and interest.

All three of these subdivisions have been successfully completed and sold and filed in the courthouse granted deeds of ownership, and a release from a promissory note is given to the now owners.

Owner-finance can be a great successful, and profitable business. This will be using the same concept and process of owner Finance and mailbox income; I will be showing you in the following chapters. For your review and a visual of the process, we have used to do the developed subdivisions.

The important thing for you to know is how to do it with a minimum investment of $30,000 dollars can bring, after expenses, a

# THE DREAMER'S DREAM

huge return of anywhere from 1,000 to 2,000% depending on what you pay for the initial cost per acre and a few more detailed factors being taken into consideration while it's being negotiated with the seller, cost of property and the sale per acre to sell to a client. I would give you step-by-step instructions to follow if you choose to do it from beginning to end.

# Chapter 4
# A New Chapter In My Life

The subdivisions were completed, a survey was done, and the roads were completed. All permits are required by legal entities. The buyers were making their monthly payments for the terms they chose, either paid for 10 years are 15 years. The payments paid directly to the Eagle Pass office or sent by mail or paid in person until paid in full.

During this time, 1 went through a divorce, which created many problems and financial hardships. I moved to San Antonio, and the employees I left behind in charge of collecting the payments saw an opportunity and embezzled $35,000 cash payments on the land paid by clients.

Once I discovered this had happened, I had to take the loss and credit all those clients for their payments. After that, I moved the accounting and note receivables to San Antonio to avoid other losses.

A new chapter opened in my life after the divorce, as I had two daughters, Mariza Casales and Erika Casales, from my earlier marriage to raise to support and educate as a single parent. I went ahead to get my real estate license so as to be licensed to legally sell

# THE DREAMER'S DREAM

houses, my insurance license to sell life insurance, and the mortgage license to be able to assist the clients with the total home purchase.

Over the next several years, I worked in real estate, putting my license under various brokers that hold the licenses of agents for a percentage of their sales, taking the main responsibility under the state. I started my own mortgage company "Global Mortgage Resources," and I had an office for 10 years in the same building. I had Real Estate, mortgages, and life insurance, and I did well, selling and serving all three entities.

In late 2003, I met my present husband, Fred Thomas Potter. He was the best thing that had happened in my life, along with my two daughters, who had moved to Austin and started their own careers, Mariza with the City of Austin and Erika working for Price, Waterhouse Cooper, and raising their own families. Fred had retired from a career in the aircraft engineering industry and moved to San Antonio from the Dallas area. He was 100% committed to helping me in my business. At that time, I continued doing Mortgages, Selling Real Estate, and life insurance.

Then in 2006, soon after the mortgage crisis occurred, Banks and lenders went out of business, and real estate and mortgage sales decreased.

Based on the decrease in sales from mortgages and real estate sales, we decided to shut down the mortgage company, and I suspended my real estate license. I kept my insurance license, and Fred obtained his license, and together we worked the insurance full-time for a few years.

We did a lot of traveling to visit clients, and it was very profitable for us. But, because of the traveling, we decided to slow down. I kept my insurance license and still make a few sales and work in the senior market doing advantage plans for the people that are going to have a 65th birthday.

Fred and I have been working side by side and have become a perfect team. We have balanced our work with each other's ability, putting together his management skills and my sales experience.

In 2008, using my land development experience along with my great partner and husband Fred, together started a new owner-financed land development in the in the outskirts of the Antonio area, near the new Toyota plant called "LAS BRISAS COUNTRY LIVING" It was developed using the same owner finance land development and mailbox income, it proved once again it be to be a successful and profitable business. By following the same process as the other three subdivisions and we followed the same basic steps as the first development in 1973, las Hacienditas, Carretas, and La Herradura, as we continued With our newest.

As you work on these projects, it gets easier to do. Once you get the hang of it, it is addictive! You work hard to put the project

## THE DREAMER'S DREAM

together for a year or two, and then after that, you sit back and enjoy the profits as you watch the money come in for seven to ten years with a HUGE return.

# Chapter 5
# The Cheap and Cheerful Project Continues

Currently, my husband and I are working on one of our latest projects. We bought fifty acres to subdivide doing the same as before, owner-financed development, sold as smaller acre tracts. We started the project in October 2020 and named it "RANCHITOS LA BAHIA," located in the Matagorda County area; we have sold 23 tracts as of March 2022. The project was divided into one and two-acre tracts. Due to the Texas state rules about septic tanks and water wells, smaller tracts of land cannot be sold; the size for a water well and septic tank the tracts must have a minimum of one & one-half acres.

The owner-financed tracts of land were done in the same manner as before by using the same concepts as earlier developments. "RANCHITOS LA BAHIA," our newest and latest project, has now been completed. It took us one year and five months from the date of land purchase for permits, surveying, etc., and the completion of sales of the land tracts.

23 tracts have been sold, and the clients are sending payments by mail; for that reason, we call these land developments

## THE DREAMER'S DREAM

a "mailbox income business."

One of the last things you need to do for your clients is to contact the county's 911 coordinator to get 911 street addresses assigned to each tract in the Subdivision. You request the telecom plat PVT for private road access. You will need to supply the proper names for your streets so it can be sent and approved by the county commissioners. Once you do a final review, you send it back to the person in charge at the county to do the final designation of addresses for each tract.

One of the last things you will need for completion and occupancy are the light poles. We used American Electric Power, as they are the electric providers in Matagorda County.

AEP electric company requires a ten (10') foot easement, and the easement must be shown on the survey you will provide the power company allowing access for installing transmission poles.

It must be a separate exhibit drawing provided by your surveyor showing a map with easement right of way.

The light poles have a cost of anywhere between $1500 to $2500 per pole, depending on your electric provider and the location of your development.

You may have to get a bank note or a loan to pay for the poles, as they require payment in full when you contract with the light company. Another option can be if you have the funds in your Company account, you can use those funds for the light poles. This should be your last major expense needed. This is needed so that clients can connect to the transmission lines and get electric service.

It is exciting and rewarding to see your development begin to blossom as clients begin to move into their newly bought manufactured homes or break ground for the home of their dreams.

Over the next few chapters, I will give you detailed step-by-step how to do land development. I will share my knowledge, my secrets, and my experiences to achieve a successful outcome as we have done. The concept we have followed in the other subdivisions has been the same process; the only changes to follow are according to the locations and the rules and regulations of the area. Based on the earlier information, I am sure you will want to know the processes as how it works end, how to go about in getting started and avoiding some of the headaches in the process, and minimize unnecessary expenses before you take it to completion and start enjoying your profits.

# Chapter 6
# Scouting to Find Your Land

This kind of development has a huge effect on your investment. The return can be anywhere from 1000% to 2000% after expenses depending on the cost of the land (acreage) that you bought and after expenses, and the sale of the tracts once surveyed. I will show you the summary and basics of the first investment, after expenses and profits on our last project, these will give you a better understanding of how the land development process works. The return of your investment is compared to the return of oil well royalties. The return of your investment is received after the notes of the property and development expenses are paid from the proceeds of the client's payments and down payments. Our part of the 60/40 split will be received monthly for 7 to 10 years or until the client pays for his property in full.

At the end of these chapters, I will have different maps, surveys, and several visuals of one of the last projects we just completed.

In the following chapters, I will also break down the process in detail from beginning to end. I will give you a clear explanation so that you understand the exact process in case you decide to take the steps forward to do this profitable venture of owner-finance subdivisions with "mail-box income."

# FRANCES CASALES POTTER

Before you start anything, you must do your due diligence in checking the demographics of the areas that you might think are a good target for this kind of project. Small towns are ideal where there is a need for affordable housing outside of city limits. Stay away from larger cities and towns as they tend to have more restrictions. The best locations are usually found in the rural areas of the county. Things to consider,

1. Population
2. Industry
3. Employment
4. Factories
5. The number of people working there and how many are being hired in those areas.

This is extremely important because the working people are going to be your buyers. People with good salaries, with little or no credit, laborers working farms and ranches, heavy equipment operators, truck drivers, and even managers working in the factories and in the area.

All of these are the folks you will direct your marketing to. In addition to the above, look for information in places like the Chamber of Commerce and corporate human resources, interview employees that work in the area, and also talk to the restaurant owners about the area and what their housing needs are.

# THE DREAMER'S DREAM

Take the time to scout the area 15 to 20 miles from the factories or large industrial areas. The closer to the factories, the easier it will be to sell the individual land tracts.

Once you have found a suitable area that you think has potential for your project, look for the land.

Start looking for land that looks abandoned, land where the older family members have passed away, and the children or heirs are looking to get rid of the land they inherited. Most of the time, those children will negotiate because they are not interested in doing what their parents did or do not want to continue working the land.

Look for acreage with abandoned shacks, barns, houses, or old farm equipment that has not been used in years.

Go to the courthouse and look at the records, check tax foreclosures, and scout the areas looking for sale by owner signs. Contact realtors from the area that are familiar with what is selling and who is selling it. Check their listings. They may have a listing with the characteristics of what you want. Seasoned realtors know if some people are in a financial bind and are looking to sell. Check the newspaper ads in the area.

If you find a property that looks suitable, verify that there is no other project like yours in the area. Being first in anything increases your chances of being successful.

It is important that once you find a property that interests you and before you make a contract, be sure there are no drainage ditches or canals. Check with FEMA to be sure the property is not in the flood plain. Also, verify deed restrictions to ensure you can do what you want, and there are no restrictions.

You do not want to buy a property in a flood plain; I repeat, you DO NOT want to buy in a flood plain. Your clients will not be able to build, and you can be stuck with land you cannot sell.

Also, Drainage ditches, canals, rivers, and streams all have more areas of concern, such as easements and permits required by the county drainage district. Easements mean you give up land that the county requires to have access to go through to clean the canals or drainage ditches; the easements you give up take away from the land you can sell.

# Chapter 7
# Funding and Purchasing your Future Retirement

As we start to take steps to buy property, there is something you must remember. To develop a large tract, it will be the same process as a small one. This is important to remember because of the costs. There will be added costs for roads and improvements. However, your profits will be greater and will justify the extra expense. The more acres you can afford to buy, the more potential for larger profits.

If you have limited funds to start with, start with fifty acres. Take into consideration that a down payment will be needed for financing. Usually, it is about 30% of the purchase price.

The down payment will depend on your financing, a bank, or your funds for owner financing.

You will need to keep in mind; besides the first down payment, you will need funds for 3-6 months of payments and other funds for the expenses while you are putting the project together.

In addition, you will also need funds for a surveyor and land clearing. If you have limited funds and it is hard to take the liability of the first purchase, you might consider an investor willing to mafia a split with you and help with funding. Split is negotiable, but remember you are going to do ALL the leg work. I recommend a 60/40 split.

The 60% You receive would be the major percentage for being the initiator with the idea of the development and have the knowledge of the project; the 40% is the investor/Partner will be for contributing to the purchase and initial expenses as well as any other funds you will both agree on.

Remember, the investor will not get his profits until after all final expenses have been fulfilled and paid. He must understand this clearly.

A monetary draw should be paid to the managing partners for putting the project together, setting up the office, receiving payments, collections, sales, and the work needed to take the project to completion. To avoid misunderstanding, be clear that the additional 20% over his 40% is for the knowledge and experience that we brought to him into this unique land development project. By bringing the deal is an opportunity to receive a great return of investment without doing any participation in the work or involvement in the project.

If you choose to look for a partner and go this route, you will need to make a summary breakdown of the cost of acres, the selling price per acre plus an interest rate of (Approximately 8%), to be charged to the client's principal and interest included in the monthly payment for financing for 7 to 10 years, by showing the added numbers to your total it will show the complete profit and the estimated return of the investment.

The figures are calculated based on the sale to the client per acre in addition to interest; when you put both figures together, it will reflect the amount of profit you will make. Typically, this is a rate of 1000% to 2000%) returns on investment. The total is then split 60/40 to show each partner's share, as I have explained above.

Through the years, we have completed five (5) subdivisions using these concepts with a proven record of profits and successes.

By selling the land into tracts as owner finance, the clients send their payments by mail or by using an online banking app like Venmo, CASHAPP, or Zelle an online banking system, using your phone number for the client's deposits to your bank, you sign up on your computer. The payments are then deposited in your bank. Or they can pay directly in person or send by mail. The payments made monthly from your clients create a cash flow business.

When you are looking for an investor, the preceding information can be a guideline to show the investor and give them an idea of how the investment process works by showing a summary of actual numbers of the purchased expenses and after-expense profits clearly show a return of his investment and why it is worth investing.

It is a good idea to have an investor agreement or a partnership agreement in place to protect both you and your investor. Your agreement must specify clearly in detail how the investor will get compensated after expenses. You Will also need an LLC Corporation. (Limited liability corporation) to protect both parties and limit the liability of possible laws suits from a client or anyone else that could get hurt on the premises.

# Chapter 8
# Taking it to Completion: The Purchase

Once you have your investor and you have your property selected, it is time to make the deal. As you are negotiating with your landowner, it is important to remember to include the following information in the contract.

1. Purchase price per acre

2. Down payment 3. Interest rate

4. Term of contract

5. Monthly payments

6. Address to mail payments

7. Release of acreage sold

The release of the acreage needs to be given to the buyer when he completes paying for the acres in full under the terms of their contract that was purchased in installments is especially important to give the clients a release of lien when they pay off their property, to be able to do so You must have negotiated with the owner from whom you bought the property and was owner financed. The amount you pay for an acre for a release is determined by the first seller, the amount he would want for each release per acre. The amount to be paid for their releases per acre must be clear and in writing in the first document in the initial purchase with the seller.

Make sure you read the contract to be sure there is overlooked information in the small print, important items like property restrictions, liens, easements, or language that would prevent you from subdividing the property. Be sure there are no taxes owed or any other debts, and you are getting a clear title. Be sure to ask for an updated survey from the seller. A survey shows exact measurement boundaries, canals, and if it is in the flood plain.

Be sure that the payment due date is clear, requesting, if possible, 45 days (about one and a half months). This buys you time to start your project. The final date is recorded on your contract; review it thoroughly before signing.

Once this is all complete, and everyone has signed, it is time to get moving.

# Chapter 9
# Project begins The Vision of Success!

Once your purchase is complete, it is time to hire a surveyor. We recommend that you hire a local surveyor, someone from the area. A couple of reasons, one, they are familiar with the rules and regulations, and they are usually connected to local commissioners in the area; your project will move faster, is important because they be the ones to file your plat. The surveyor will break into tracts to show as individual tract sizes as required by county and state. Surveyor will Prepare plans, and once completed, he will submit to the county and environmental offices for approval. Once the surveyor has completed the plat, he must put it in Mylar (is a plastic clear sheet with all the survey information). Usually, they require an 18" X 24" size but check with the county before making an expense because it could change). He will need at least three (3) copies to send for final approval.

You will also need to include in your submission package a tax certificate (show that taxes are paid to date), and must be provided from the county tax office for a fee. The copy of the deed legal document shows the initial purchase from the seller and buyer. Once you complete the submission package, check with the Environmental offices prior to sending it, as you may have overlooked something that must be included in the package. This will help to avoid delays.

Also, have the surveyor prepare an easement exhibit for the utility company to allow the utility company to figure out the placement of light poles. The utility company engineer will need to be contacted for their information. This should be as an AutoCAD (is a plat required by the light company drawn by the surveyor) to include in the file to provide to the utility company when they send the application to the county to supply light poles to the Subdivision for power lines.

Once the platting is done (platting is a system the surveying engineers use to divide the land into individual acre tracts), once the Subdivision is approved by the county, the surveyor will place survey pins to denote property lines and easements. At this time, you can start pre-sales and begin to generate income from down payments. This will help you to pay your monthly payments and your development expenses as you progress with improvements and pre-sales.

You now need to start promoting your land tracts for sale as you continue with the development. You do this with signs on the frontage road. The sign we used was an 8-foot by a 4-foot vinyl sign on a 2' X 4' X 8' frame; placed our last project was along the road near the entrance so people passing by would see it. Advertising works! An eye-catching visual sign attracts curiosity and creates

## THE DREAMER'S DREAM

sales.

It is best to use the same name on your signs for your development that you used when you bought the property, also the same one that was used to open the bank account. For the development. (Clients like ranch names associated with their culture) You may order a large vinyl sign with your name from an affordable sign company (we used Signs.com). Make sure the letters on the sign are brightly colored with the subdivision name. Include, For Sale by Owner, "Owner Financed," and "2-5-acre Tracts," and make sure the letters show up well. Make sure to include a phone number where it is high enough to be visible to clients.

You will need to clear the land and burn the brush. Before you start burning the brush, you will need to contact the local fire department for permission to burn the piles. You can usually find local labor to help you do the clearing of land. The next step is cutting of the roads so that your buyers will have access to the property.

The roads by now may already have been platted, as shown in the survey; for the maintainers and heavy equipment to know where they are to go cut the road. by asking people if they know someone who can mow or grade or cut roads; there is always someone of our clients that know guys that work on the nearby farms, their bosses let them use the heavy equipment to do our roads when they are not too busy in their jobs. These people know how to grade and put top down, and it helps us to lower the construction cost.

# Chapter 10
# Marketing Begins Sales and Cash Flow

You will initially begin to get a lot of phone calls. Always keep their name and number so you can get back to them. Some will be calling out of curiosity. Give them just enough information so they will meet you at the property. You will more than likely have to make several trips to show it. Of Course, You can list with a realtor; however, you should sell the property yourself instead of listing it with a realtor. Yes, they will help to market the property, but they are going to want commissions from 2% to 6%, and that will decrease your return on your investment. In marketing your development, you need exposure. You started with the signs. Now you need to create flyers to identify the Subdivision so use the same name as you used to open a bank account and other legal documents, and put in the flyer information as to phone and location to be contacted for the showings.

Once you have flyers, start putting them in restaurants, gas stations, convenience stores, furniture rentals, and mobile home sales wherever you find a bulletin board or wall to stick them on.

Word of mouth from clients will pass the word from relatives to friends to coworkers and so on.

As people drive by and see progress on the land and see the

signs, they will stop and ask questions and your sales opportunity arises. Always ask for a referral from your clients or the grocery clerk, or the waiter at the restaurant where you eat. They are all prospects.

# Chapter 11
# The Documents

This is one of the most important parts of the whole program, The Legal documents in order. As soon as possible, before you sell anything, you need to get your "DOCS IN A ROW" One of the best places to find what you will need is Legal Zoom, or other legal aid sites, that can help you with the documents you will need to complete the sale and protect you and your client's rights. They are as follows:

1. The Deed of Trust, this is what gives the client his ownership interest.
2. The Warranty Deed with Vendor's Lien is what protects your (the seller's) interest and ensures you get paid on the note the buyer owes on the property
3. The Promissory Note specifies the terms of the financing, the interest rate, tells the client when it was purchased location, and the terms for how long they will make payments.
4. The Deed of Trust and Warranty Deed with Vendor's Lien both must be signed and notarized before you file in the county where a property has been purchased. You do not need to file the Promissory note you retain in clients' records;

you will retain it until the note is paid in full; you will then give the note and release of lien to the client.

5. The Warranty Deed and The Deed of Trust must describe the property in the Metes and Bounds that outlines the property boundaries and legal description as shown in the survey plat.

It is important you specify in the contract that the land is being sold "AS IS" with no improvements; the water well and septic systems are the buyer's responsibility. The client must follow state rules and regulations in the construction of the septic tank and water well.

The contract you, as the developer, put together will have some restrictions to protect the Subdivision. For example, you include in the contracts the following, no wildfowl (chickens, turkey, ducks, etc.), no pigs, no cars on blocks or in unrepaired condition, and mobile homes are allowed. However, they cannot be older than ten years and must be skirted within 180 days (about 6 months). These are a few samples of deed restrictions to put in your contracts to keep the Subdivision clean and looking good. The promissory note is just that, a promise from the buyer to pay the note for the property. It includes the buyers' names, addresses, and phone numbers. It will show the amount of the down payment and the amount financed. This includes the interest rate and the number of payments. It will tell them the due date, the amount of monthly payment, and the date of the

# THE DREAMER'S DREAM

final payment. It is an open-ended contract which means they can pay it off at any time without penalty.

# Chapter 12
# The Sales Contract The Best Part of the Project

By now we have given you a lot of information to prepare you to get to this point. To be able to have your client in front of you and she/he is ready to make the purchase. We have explained the process so that you are able and ready to seal the deal with the buyer. You should fill out the Deed of Trust, The Warranty Deed with the Vendor's lien, and the promissory note while they are in front of you; the final process is to have both parties sign the (client/seller) property manager or owner in front of a notary public. NOTE: The County will not let you record unnotarized documents. And they must be signed in the location of the county the Subdivision is located in front of a Notary Public. All contracts must have a Grantee, who is the buyer who receives the deed.

The Grantor is the seller, the one who gives the deed to the buyer. Clearly specified legal description and a copy of the plat for that tract.

In the contract, You should use the name of your Limited Partnership as the property owner of the Subdivision and you as the manager of the limited Partnership.

# THE DREAMER'S DREAM

Once agreements are signed and you have been given the down payment, you will need to give copies of all the documents and a receipt for the down payment.

We usually give the buyers six pre-addressed envelopes so they can mail the first 6 initial payments. We also give them the information for paying through one of the apps mentioned earlier (Venmo, Zelle, CashApp).

However, it is safer for them to send a money order by mail. A receipt of their payment will be sent back as soon as received.

You will then take the original Deed and Warranty Deed with Vendor's Lien to the County Clerk in the county where your property is located and file it. This provides a legal record of the transaction. You also will take it to the tax accessor's office to have the property taxes under their name.

You do not need to file the Promissory note. However, if you choose to do so, you can. If you decide you are going to file, it must be notarized.

There is a fee for each page, another company expense. You just sold your first property; from now on, you show the property, make the sales, proceed to fill out documents, get them notarized, file with the county district clerk and follow the process we have taught you, repeat until you have sold them all. The Cash Flow begins!

# Chapter 13
# Tracking Your Sales And Client Payments

One of the first steps to carefully track a client's payment is to set up a filing system. The best way to do it is by tract number. For example, Mary Smith purchased tract #1, so Mary smith will be the first file. Even if Mary Smith was not the first person to Purchase a tract, she bought a tract one.

You will then file each purchaser in the numerical order of tracts, number one, number two, and so on.

Your next step and this is critical, is to set up your Excel files. It is a computer program that you use to set up in Quick Books so that you may accurately track your postings for payments received, breaks interest, and principal. This will safeguard you and your client to ensure accurate accounting of payments.

You will keep a copy of the deposit, the check, the receipt, and the envelope in each client's file.

The money orders sent by the client can be deposited in many ways, by sending a deposit slip and the money order by mail to the bank, by using the bank's online deposit system to take a picture of the check/money order, and by depositing it online. Or take it to the bank in person. We recommend using electronic deposit when possible. Also, you can have your client send the deposit via Venmo or Zelle if your bank accepts this form of payment.

All payments must have a receipt mailed to the client, no matter which way you choose to deposit.

You can track clients mailing by subscribing to the USPS tracking, a great app that will notify you each day what mail is coming that day. That way, you will know what to expect in your mailbox.

From this point on, all the work is behind you. All you do is make deposits and enjoy the fruits of your labor. It will take about a year to two years to get to this point, and you will still have some obligations like land payments and miscellaneous payments depending on how much you borrowed for expenses, but your investment should start paying for itself, and you will not have a worry. Occasionally as part of the business, you may need to remind a client of their payments

However, the mailbox money as part of the book's title fits perfect; people send land payments by mail, and you deposit daily to the company's bank account. How Awesome is that?

# Chapter 14
# It All Comes Together

As I approach the end of my book, I wish to emphasize the fantastic opportunity my information is for an individual that is seriously interested in exploring the entrepreneurship of affordable land development with a minimal cash investment. I am sharing with you fifty years of my personal land development experience by providing you with a detailed step-by-step informational road map to a great business opportunity to help you achieve your dream of financial independence and comfortable retirement like we have. It is not that hard to do if you take care of and follow instructions. This is not to say you may have things that are different, but those are the unimportant things that may change in the process, and you will adjust. Remember that to succeed, you must take the first step and then the second step, and so on, until you finally reach your goal.

## SOME FINAL THOUGHTS

At the beginning of this book, I gave you a bio of myself to give you an idea of what a young, hard-working immigrant girl can do if only we get the opportunity.

It was never in my wildest dreams that affordable developments would give us the financial freedom in my life to travel all over Mexico and Europe, to have nice jewelry, cars, and two homes, and be able to assist my daughters with their educations and purchase their homes, and to assist my parents with their financial needs.

The affordable owner-financed developments have made it possible for me to reach the "DREAMER'S DREAM" We hope it can help you too!

FRANCES CASALES POTTER

# SUBDIVISION PLATS

1. LAS HACIENDITAS     1973
2. LAS CARRETAS     1977
3. LA HERRADURA     1978
4. LAS BRISAS     2008
5. RANCHITOS LA BAHIA     2020

# THE DREAMER'S DREAM

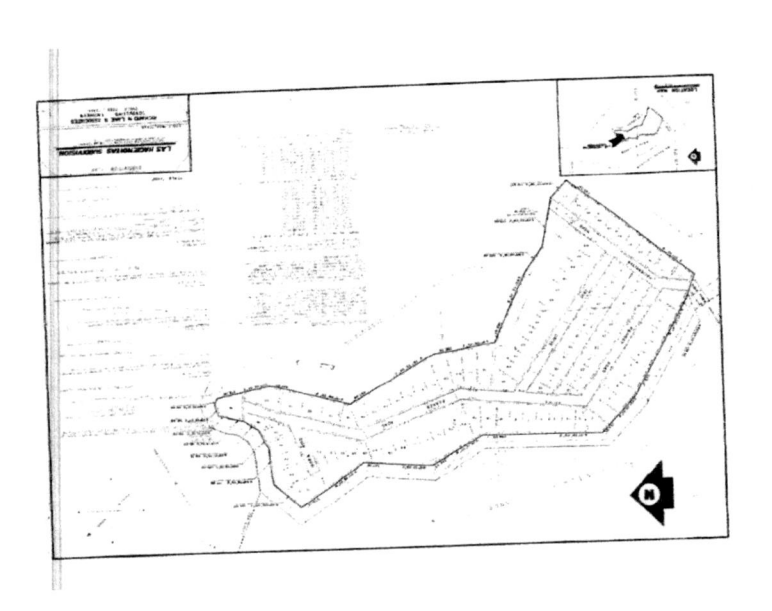

**LAS HACIENDITAS**

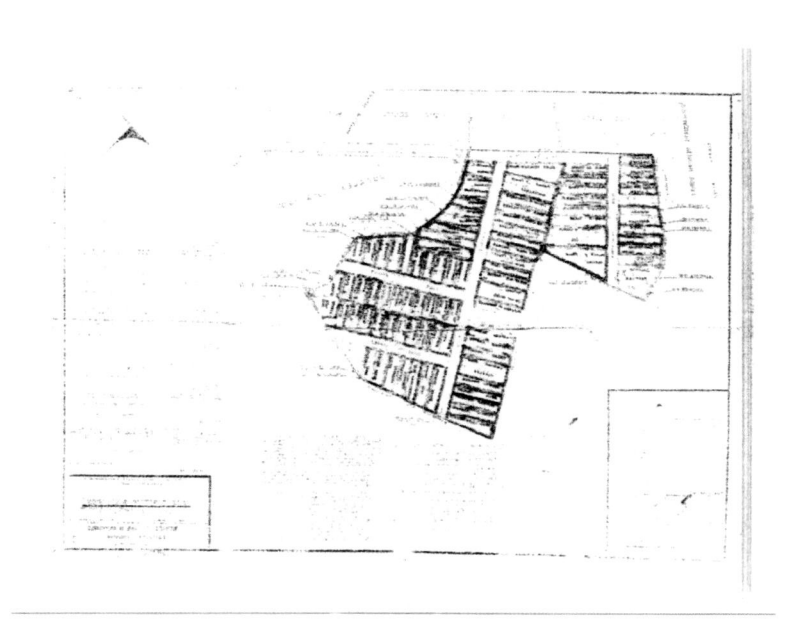

**LAS CARRETAS**

# THE DREAMER'S DREAM

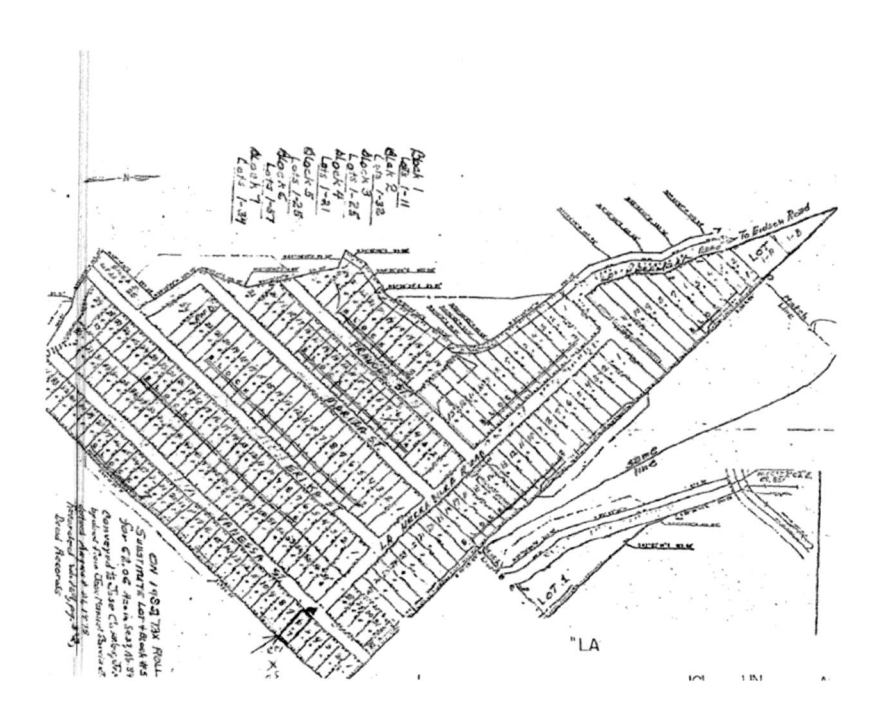

**LA HERRADURA**

# FRANCES CASALES POTTER

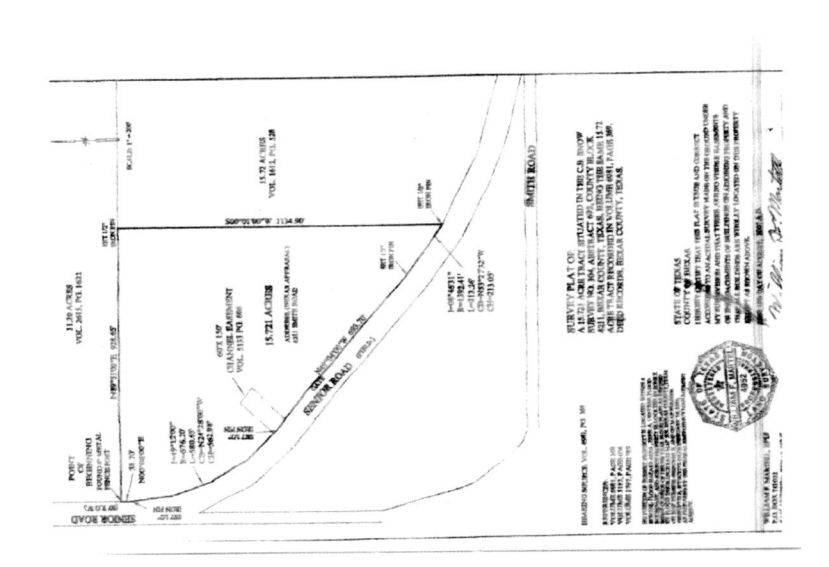

**LAS BRISAS**

# THE DREAMER'S DREAM

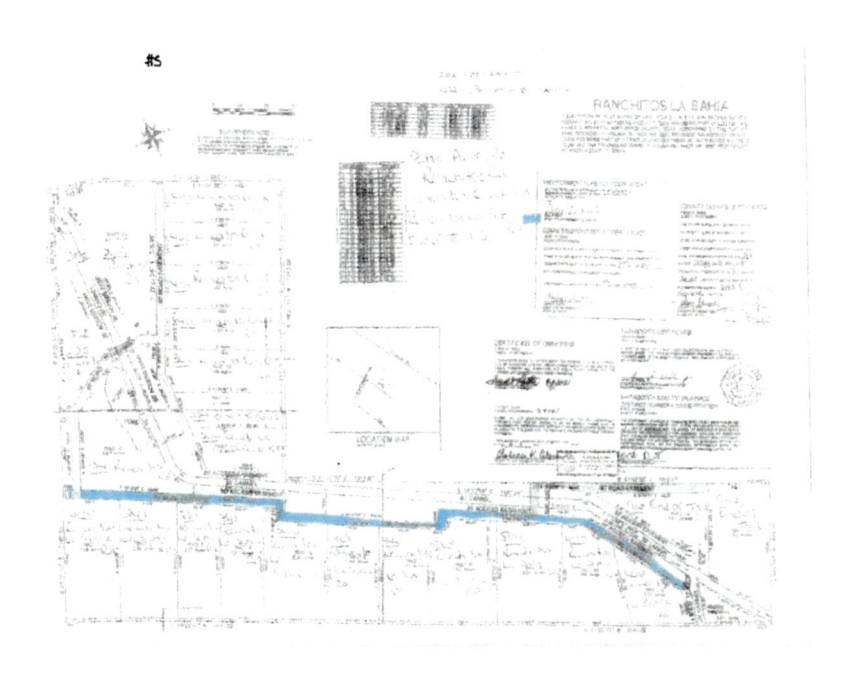

**RANCHITOS LA BAHIA**

FRANCES CASALES POTTER

# SUMMARYs OF INVESTMENT ANALYSIS

**INITIAL INVESTMENT PER PARTNER (2)**

**PARTNERS**

**CASH**       $20,000.00

**BANK**       $5,000.00

**(3) PAYMENTS OF $2,185.05**

   **TOTAL*: $27,185.05**

*THIS IS JUST AN EXAMPLE BASED ON OUR LAST PROJECT)

**INITIAL LAND INVESTMENT: $197,500.00**

**DOWN PAYMENT:**            $ 40,000.00

**PAYMENTS FOR 10 YEARS:**   $ 1,456.70

# THE DREAMER'S DREAM

THE AUTHORS DURING COVID-19
AT ENTRANCE SIGN

FRANCES CASALES POTTER

ROAD CLEARING FRONT TRACT #23
RANCHITOS LA BAHIA

# THE DREAMER'S DREAM

VIEW TRACT #23

RANCHITOS LA BAHIA

FRANCES CASALES POTTER

SOLD SIGN TRACT #11
RANCHITOS LA BAHIA

# THE DREAMER'S DREAM

SOLD SIGN TRACT #10
RANCHITOS LA BAHIA

# FRANCES CASALES POTTER

BURNING BRUSH
RANCHITOS LA BAHIA

# THE DREAMER'S DREAM

MORE BRUSH BURNING

RANCHITOS LA BAHIA

# FRANCES CASALES POTTER

LAND CLEARING - RANCHITOS LA BAHIA

## THE DREAMER'S DREAM

*LAND VIEW - RANCHITOS LA BAHIA*

BURNING DEBRIS TRACT #21,22
RANCHITOS LA BAHIA

# THE DREAMER'S DREAM

CLEARING AND BURNING
TRACT #11.12.13
RANCUITOS LA BAHIA

FRANCES CASALES POTTER

**COUNTRY LIVING**
BUILD YOUR OWN HOME
JUST A FEW MINUTES FROM THE CITY
CLOSE TO ELEMENTARY AND MIDDLE SCHOOLS
3.75 + ACRE TRACTS
OWNER FINANCE
NO CREDIT CHECK

FOR ADDITIONAL INFORMATION

CALL

210-218-2663

210-259-1575

FLYER FOR LAS BRISAS

# THE DREAMER'S DREAM

# FRANCES CASALES POTTER

# THE DREAMER'S DREAM

Made in the USA
Columbia, SC
27 July 2024

f1812a14-7a01-4d01-83a5-156da5214ea5R02